THE MORNING AFTER

Survivor of Sexual & Spiritual Abuse

E. Keysha L. Stewart-Conard
Mental Health Therapist, MA

©2021 E. Keysha L. Stewart-Conard

All Rights Reserved.

ISBN: 9798728505587

Steward Publishing, LTD.

🌐 stewardpublishing.org

No part of this book may be reproduced, stored in a retrieval system or transmitted by any means without written permission from the publisher except for brief quotations in critical reviews or articles. Unless otherwise noted, Scripture quotations are from the King James Version, New King James Version and New International Version. Used by Permission. Scripture quotations marked ESV are from the English Standard Bible Copyright. Scripture quotations marked NLT are from the New Living Translation Bible. Scripture quotations marked AMP are from The Amplified Bible. Scripture quotations marked MSG are from The Message Bible. Copyright © 1954, 1958, 1962, 1964, 1965, 1987 by The Lockman Foundation. All Rights Reserved. Used by permission.

DEDICATION

I want to dedicate this book to everyone who has ever been mishandled, misused, or mistreated, physically abused, sexually abused, verbally, or emotionally by Church leadership, authority figures, or anyone you have trusted.

DISCLAIMER

This book is written from my perspective and personal experiences, names of churches have been changed along with names of everyone involved in order to protect their privacy.

TABLE OF CONTENTS

Foreword 9
Introduction 19
Chapter 1: In The Beginning 23
Chapter 2: The Church Hats 27
Chapter 3: The Church Is Losing Its True Purpose 31
Chapter 4: Church History. 35
Chapter 5: The Best Thing I've Ever Encountered 39
Chapter 6: Being The First Female Drummer. 43
Chapter 7: It's All Just A Game. 51
Chapter 8: A Test Of My Integrity 55
Chapter 9: Rickenbacker Base (Columbus, Ohio). 61
Chapter 10: Keysha, Are You Alright?. 67
Chapter 11: I Looked Back One Last Time 73
Chapter 12: The Encounter 79
Chapter 13: Why Go Back After
    God Told You To Leave? 85

Chapter 14: I Won't Be Silent No More!.................87

Chapter 15: Start Talking My Friend...................91

Chapter 16: In Retrospect 99

References 103

FOREWORD

As a child there are three places in life that you should always feel protected: at home, at church and at school. These are places that we as adults undoubtedly assume are safe for our children. Unfortunately, these three places are at times where we are protected the least.

In THE MORNING AFTER, Keysha takes us on a journey and exposes that the place that should have been a safe haven, turned out to be a place that taught her not to trust, to second guess herself and the source for much confusion during most of her life. Experiencing this type of trauma can paralyze you and keep you stuck; allowing no room for self-growth.

Emotional, Sexual and Spiritual abuse... which is the worse? Keysha has experienced all three and they have followed her and have left many unanswered questions. The impact of this type of pain can cause you to become delusional and it's not until you lay down and go to sleep thinking that it was all a horrible joke or a bad dream and wake up and believing it will be all over. Well not the case. It was THE MORNING AFTER that what she thought was not real became her daily reality. The people whom she trusted the most are the ones who betrayed her. Not just the ones who committed the acts of abuse, but even more devastating were the ones to whom she reached out for help and yet abandoned her. Unfortunately, this happens more often than we think, and most don't have a triumphant ending.

In THE MORNING AFTER, Keysha was able to take the pain that she endured for over thirty-five years and use them as stepping stones to grow, heal and now help others to move forward in their lives. What the devil meant for evil, God worked it out for her good. As you read each page see the pain and the strength that has propelled Keysha to being whole and healed.

On a more personal note...

In the spring of 2001, I was not given the opportunity to stand with you as you tried to tell your story of spiritual and sexual abuse as you lumped me with everyone else thinking that I would not support you because of my relationship with your accused abuser. I publicly take this opportunity to say that I believe you now and I believed you then. I also apologize to you for those who turned their back on you leaving you vulnerable and uncovered and presented you as an outcast to the church. Keysha, I am so proud of you for telling your truth and having a front row seat cheering you on as you continue to heal.

Alaina Holloway—Carpenter
January 30, 2020

MY PURPOSE

My purpose for writing this book is to let those who have been hurt by church leadership or church authority or any person of great influence in the church or in any capacity, to understand and know that we are working for and living with flawed individuals who just so happen to be called by God. Often times we make the mistake of forgetting that because a person is called to be a Pastor, Bishop, Teacher, Evangelist, or even a Prophet or any position in the church or been provided some type of authority over you, that they will not make mistakes and that they will not fall. However, it is when those who are chosen, forget that they are human and fail to acknowledge their frailties and admit their mistakes.

THE MORNING AFTER

It's so weird that when a person gets higher in God accountability is null and void; or so it seems. The requirement to repent and be humble no longer becomes a part of the "job description". It becomes more about how big the church is, or how many members they have. I thought honesty and living Holy and being set a part was the way. When did it no longer become the responsibility of those who lead us that they can make this a requirement for the congregants to stay celibate, and instructing us to wait on God, but they can have a wife and a few women in the church on the side to sleep with; or they can have women planted in different states where they preach to sleep with or have these women planted in different areas of the world? It's shocking and heartbreaking at the same time. Unfortunately, it does happen.

We also have to remember, that God knows all, He sees all, and if there is no person on earth to tell you that He will vindicate you in due time, I am telling you now through this book that God is your vindicator. If you are not a believer in God, I am speaking to whatever higher power you believe in. For me, it is and will always be God, Jesus who is my Lord and Savior.

Psalm 35:24 (NIV) tells, "Vindicate me in your righteousness, LORD my God; do not let them gloat over me." Also, Romans 12:19 (KJV)

"Dearly beloved, avenge not yourselves, but rather give place unto wrath: for it is written, Vengeance is mine; I will repay, saith the Lord".

I have been a victim of abuse on and off for close to 36 years. I can't remember a time when abuse was not a part of my life. I should be either dead, in jail, or in a room with four walls and a straight- jacket. I am no longer a victim, but a survivor, and my testimony is being told not from a victim's perspective, but a survivor's perspective. I live as a witness to say that God is a keeper of the mind, soul and body. I had known the Lord as early as the age of eight years old, and it has been the Lord that has been a constant in my life. He has kept me and protected me even now, as recovery for me is a day-by-day opportunity. I say opportunity because I am a firm believer that what doesn't kill you, makes you strong and allows you the chance to tell another of your experience.

Being a survivor of abuse means that now you have the power and anointing to help another. Now you can reach back and snatch someone else from the pain of abuse or simply walk through it with them. Doing this can cause you to be afraid of what you see, and what you may come in contact with. Do not be afraid of another person's pain. Seeing someone else's pain can make you step back, because the reaction you receive from them will not be towards you personally. Most times when I was lashing out at people for trying to help me it was a defense mechanism. It was used to protect me from being harmed.

To those who are a survivor of abuse, we are charged now to help those who are still struggling. It is through the love of Christ and His compassion that allows us to see another's pain and go forward in being that bridge and not to leave them in it alone. Just like a doula is by the side of a mother giving birth, so are you, survivor, by the side of your sister, brother, friend or someone you may not even know.

The scriptures that give me comfort in knowing that even though I was abused, I still do not stand in the place of God to judge my abusers.

Jeremiah 23:1-12 (KJV)

[1] Woe be unto the pastors that destroy and scatter the sheep of my pasture! saith the Lord.

THE MORNING AFTER

² Therefore thus saith the Lord God of Israel against the pastors that feed my people; Ye have scattered my flock, and driven them away, and have not

visited them: behold, I will visit upon you the evil of your doings, saith the Lord.

³ And I will gather the remnant of my flock out of all countries whither I have driven them and will bring them again to their folds; and they shall be fruitful and increase.

⁴ And I will set up shepherds over them which shall feed them: and they shall fear no more, nor be dismayed, neither shall they be lacking, saith the Lord.

⁵ Behold, the days come, saith the Lord, that I will raise unto David a righteous Branch, and a King shall reign and prosper, and shall execute judgment and justice in the earth.

⁶ In his days Judah shall be saved, and Israel shall dwell safely: and this is his name whereby he shall be called, The Lord Our Righteousness.

⁷ Therefore, behold, the days come, saith the Lord, that they shall no more say, The Lord liveth, which brought up the children of Israel out of the land of Egypt;

⁸ But, The Lord liveth, which brought up and which led the seed of the house of Israel out of the north country, and from all countries whither I had driven them; and they shall dwell in their own land.

⁹ Mine heart within me is broken because of the prophets; all my bones shake; I am like a drunken man, and like a man whom wine hath overcome, because of the Lord, and because of the words of his holiness.

¹⁰ For the land is full of adulterers; for because of swearing the land mourneth; the pleasant places of the wilderness are dried up, and their course is evil, and their force is not right.

¹¹ For both prophet and priest are profane; yea, in my house have I found their wickedness, saith the Lord.

¹² Wherefore their way shall be unto them as slippery ways in the darkness: they shall be driven on and fall therein: for I will bring evil upon them, even the year of their visitation, saith the Lord.

My Desire for You...

So, in the meantime, ma'am or sir your job is to heal. Heal so this part of you can be used to help others overcome what you have overcome. Heal so that the pain you see that's familiar in someone else does not scare you away from helping them.

My prayer for each person that reads this book is that you begin your journey to healing, or if you have already started, that you continue in the process that you become strong, vigilant and fearless in letting others know your story. You may say that you don't want to talk to anyone about what happened to you because that's just not for you. That's ok, but go seek help, find a good therapist to help you walk through this trauma. Most importantly, always remember that a secret loses its power once it's told. What's your secret?

INTRODUCTION

Understanding the behavior of those who have been abused

Studies show that victims of abuse from childhood, like me, can suffer much personality wise. According to Psychology Today, the development of a child's brain grows rapidly in the first few years. It is when the brain suffers from trauma during those years of development, like physical abuse, that can have lasting negative outcomes.

When someone has been abused as a child their brain is rerouted and new pathways burned into their mind. A child's brain is already a delicate thing. When the young mind has suffered from abuse, it changes the thinking patterns and operation of a healthy, normal brain. Once abuse carries over to adulthood, it can cause a great amount of consequences. They can suffer from Social Difficulties, Impulsive Behavior, Become Underachievers, and can become Depressed and Anxious, Development of poor Emotional Intelligence, struggles with intimacy, and can develop aggression and Misbehavior.

Let me be clear on what's been stated. This is not the personality of everyone that has suffered abuse. Abuse or another way of saying it is, a crime against your body, can come in several ways. I am not claiming that because you have suffered abuse, or a crime against your body, you will suffer from these symptoms, but is it most likely some do, while others may not. I highly doubt that if anyone has suffered from sexual abuse that they do not have some type of issue, relationally or otherwise. What I will say is it is typically those who suffer from abuse from childhood on to adulthood that this type of behavior can be displayed.

"On average, there are victims (age 12 or older) of rape and sexual assault each year in the United States." www.rainn.org. I am certain this number has changed since this book, but these numbers will not go down unless we start speaking up and holding people who do this accountable.

I was afraid of my abusers; it took me years to come out and share the molestation I experienced as a child and being sexually assaulted as a young adult. I was afraid of what they would think or what they would say or how this book would affect them and the people in their lives. Would I be believed? I am a nobody in the eyes of those who believe in him. I have no power, no prestige, no name, who would even listen to me if I did decide to tell?, who would I even talk to?, but after the fear of all that left me, I could care less what any of them think or how the hell they feel.

I have the support of those who have experienced sexual abuse and have gone before me. I stand on their

shoulders I declare... IT HAPPENED TO ME TOO. I was told that I am a liar, I was isolated from those I thought were my friends, because he is a "man of God" and "how dare you put your mouth on him and accuse him of doing something like that?" This type of thinking is what kept me in mental bondage for years, because it was my fear that because of who he is, he's above doing something like this, and because of who I am, I am looked at as the one deceiving or lying.

The Boy David

There's a story in the bible that I will paraphrase. The story tells of a boy going up against the giant, Goliath. The boy David was just that, a boy. Small, insignificant according to his brothers and his father. Until one day, the boy David

THE MORNING AFTER

saw the giant harassing the people of the land. He heard him ranting and raving, "I am too strong for you", You will never win, who here can defeat me?" The giant goes on to say. The boy being all but 6 feet and the giant was well over 9 feet tall, clearly the odds were against the boy David. The power was imbalanced, the boy was not a match for such a powerful Giant. He believed he could defeat the giant, but how? You ask. The boy David decided within himself, I will take five smooth stones and then declares to the giant, "I will kill you with your own weapon". The boy David tells the Giant Goliath, today! You die, you will no longer be a threat to me or the people in this land. The boy David runs to the line, swings his sling shot with the smooth stone. The stone lands in the forehead of the Giant, knocking him unconscious. The boy David then takes the sword of the Giant and cuts off his head. The moral of the story? Giants do fall, it just takes them longer...

CHAPTER 1

In the Beginning

I have been in the church pretty much all my life. I have memories dating back to when my mom used to clean the church and she would take my sister and I to help her. My sister didn't like it so much but as for me it really didn't matter. I remember feeling a closeness to God and being taught respect for His presence. I remember when my mom used to clean or when she was going to vacuum the Pulpit she would always stop and pray before the alter. What she whispered to God? I don't know but watching her instilled in me that God is to be reverenced in all things, even when cleaning the church.

My mom, aunts and grandmother are the ones who trained and raised my cousins and I in the choir and just being servants altogether in the House of the Lord. At the age of ten or eleven, I can remember singing in the choir. I can even remember being a part of the praise team or the choir from childhood, all the way into my teens and on to early adulthood.

I believe they wanted to call us the "Conard singers". It was fun while we were in it, many of my cousins and I know how to sing and so my aunts and mom thought it would be a good idea to start a group. Little did they know, we weren't as committed as they were coming up. My mom and her sisters used to sing, and on my Dad's side they play instruments. I even have an Uncle who is a former member of the Kinsmen Jazz Band.

I can remember one time I was driving home, and I felt the Lord tell me that I can do many things; that it was up to me to decide what I wanted to do. At that moment I felt this power come over me that I still to this day cannot explain; I felt empowered or something, like I had super powers and had the ability to do whatever I wanted to do supernaturally; that feeling has never left me.

Like many families, we were a chosen family, full of gifts and talents. I am one of many talents; one talent manifested at the age of maybe ten years old or younger to play

THE MORNING AFTER

the drums; because I didn't have drums, I can remember using pots and pans and toothbrushes as my first drum set.

It wasn't until my freshmen year in Akron University when I saw a girl on the drums playing at Akron University's Gospel Choir, that let me know that I can play the drums even if I am a girl.

CHAPTER 2

The Church Hats

Have you ever walked into a church and you see a row of church hats? Each woman polished, poised and smelling all good, but underneath that hat she hides a terrible secret. She hides insecurities a mile long. She's asking herself if I wore the right shoes with this outfit, or will I have on the latest. The pain in her eyes is being covered by this big ole hat she wears. Or some have just gone completely numb of what to feel. They walk around like robots on auto response. You ask them how they are doing? They automatically say, "Fine, how are you?" That hat to me is just like the masks we wear in church. Each person picking up their "mask" or their "hat" as they enter the "house of the lawd" and once they leave, they take it off and go deal with their pain silently.

THE MORNING AFTER

Some deal with it in extra marital affairs, some deal with it in shopping, or gossip, some deal with it in sexual promiscuity, some deal with it fantasizing about being with another woman, or another man or both at the same time. Some cut themselves, some drink, a whole lot of them lie to themselves and to others, and some just check out altogether. The lights are on, but there is a deadness behind the eyes and that smile. I call this being totally disconnected. This is all in hope that the pain goes away.

In all honesty, the pain increases and starts a slow death to the insides of its victim. Gnawing at your heart, then the lungs, and finally the brain. Leaving the body full of pain and this is the filter you respond out of. Your responses no longer match the questions being asked. Because the pain you hide has become visible to others and destructive to you like a cancer; so, you go on until you are the walking dead. Dead to the concerns of others, dead to the compassion of others, numb to their voices of concern, dead to the touch of others. Comatose, taking more than a defibrillator to jump start your heart to beat again, or to make you feel again.

The church hats or masks cover up a lot. They are worn for many reasons. Church has taught me how to cover up.

THE MORNING AFTER

How to pretend everything is ok by the clothes you wear, by the position you hold or by how well you keep secrets.

So far, in all my church experiences, it was rare that a person would find a leader to take someone under his/her wing and cultivate the gifts without feeling jealous, or envious, or entitled. Unfortunately, it has been my experience. I did not encounter many leaders who were committed to cultivating me properly. I seemingly was always under an insecure, leader. Often times this would lead to me being overlooked, mishandled, ignored or mistreated.

CHAPTER 3

The Church is Losing Its True Purpose

After the time of being sexually assaulted, healing was not my goal, nor was it something I'd even considered, it was getting revenge. I plotted and planned how I would get revenge on those who mishandled me and abused me. Being sexually assaulted was one of many events that led me to being fed up with trusting those who are supposed to be a representative of Christ or allow church to be a "safe space". Maybe it's unfair to place that much pressure on a flawed human being. Maybe in the twenty-first century church, you are no longer expected to be treated like you are human, but instead you are treated like if you don't make every service, or if you are not committed as much, your worth and value depreciates.

The church today has lost its fire and purpose. This disappointment has made it extremely difficult for churches that truly seek to be what Christ's mission was for its people and the church as a whole.

My Eight-Year-Old Mind

I have learned that when you are violated as a child, your boundaries are shot. It takes someone to tell you that's wrong or someone to show you the proper way or to help readjust your boundaries and thinking. Like with me. When I was eight years old, I was being molested by a family member, it was on and off from the age of 8-12 years old. My eight-year-old mind couldn't understand what was being done to me, to even understand why it was being done, so I blacked out, and came to in a different place. I remember being in the basement, but then I don't remember getting to my room.

To be even more transparent, I don't remember being penetrated, but I remember being placed on the slab like cattle and being told to "make those sounds that women make". I totally didn't get it. It's funny, the mind, and what it does to protect you. As a child you are supposed to be protected and cared for by the adults you were born to, but at that moment, at the age of eight years old, my mind was being re-wired, my body was being exposed to something an eight-year-old girl should never be exposed to. My molester chose when it was time for me to be exposed to sex, pornography and inappropriate touches far too soon. It rewires you into thinking that what's going on with you is ok and that it's "normal".

It's unfair to learn so early in life the evil that's in this world, and to be an involuntary participant of someone's deviant plan to expose an innocent child to something it's mind cannot comprehend. Abuse of any kind, sexual abuse, verbal abuse, physical abuse, emotional abuse, mental abuse. Who told them it was ok to hurt me, who told them it was alright to violate me at such a young age? What makes it ok? What in the mind of the molester makes you think that its ok to do this to vulnerable children?

CHAPTER 4

Church History

BEGINNERS LIFE CHURCH

In 1996, Beginners Life Church, there I was in the choir, young, strengthening my skill on the drums and enjoying the Lord. Things at Beginners Life Church was good, I was a teen, age 16 and looking to higher education one day in the near future. At this church there was two drummers and we were on a rotation schedule. It seemed most Sundays when it was my turn if the main drummer wanted to play, regardless if it was his Sunday or not, he was allowed to play.

This one particular Sunday he wanted to play, the choir was singing, and he was sitting in the front row motioning for me to get up, so he can come play. I refused to get up and so I kept playing. He got upset and told the first lady of the church who then looked at me and motioned to me "GET UP" and said something like, "what's wrong with you" If he wants to play, you let him play. My heart was broken; because I joined the church with my family, it would be out of order to leave because I was still a minor and under my mother's rule. So, from that time till the day I left, if the main drummer wanted to play, he played.

One time at Beginners Life Church they had a daycare. I used to work with the Head Teacher who was married to one of the Pastor's sons, let's call him "Delroy". He would come around often to talk to his wife which was natural. It was one afternoon when the head teacher was in the office and I was in the classroom, Delroy comes in to ask me a question, but after he asked the question he froze and just stood there looking at me. His face got closer and closer to mine and he went in to kiss me on my lips. I pushed his face away and told him "no way". He apologized over and over and said to please not to tell his wife. I promised him that I wouldn't mention it to her only if he promises never to try that again; because you know being molested as a child, you are good at keeping secrets. So Delroy agreed, and we went on with our day as if nothing happened. For me, that was the final straw. When I turned eighteen years old, I went off to Akron University, and I decided I no longer wanted to be a part of Beginners Life Church.

UNITED STONE CREEK CHURCH

The year was 1997, I was finally of age to make my own decisions on where I wanted to go to church, I left Beginners Life and started visiting United Stone Creek Church or USCC with a couple of friends of mine. They were already members of USCC and knew what happened at BLC, so I started going to church with them. They were former members of Beginners Life Church as well. The preaching was good, and the people seemed very friendly. I was still a young person, so the young people were cordial and friendly. At this church, they believed in having Youth Pastor's or Parrish Pastors. The Youth pastor was about my age at the time I became a member. On the day I joined it was so scary for me. The praise and worship team were rockin' and the service was flowing nicely. The sermon was already preached, and the altar call was the last thing to be made.

I wanted so badly to walk to the altar, but I was still a bit shy and didn't really know anyone but my friend and her family; because they were already members, I was going to have to walk down that aisle by myself. Heart beating so

THE MORNING AFTER

fast, sweaty palms, and almost paralyzed I stood up to walk down the aisle to join United Stone Creek Church (USCC). The Bishop greeted me and said, "Hey Kaye". That day a new name had been given, I would no longer be called Keysha, but "Kaye". Little did I know that day was going to be the best and worst day of the rest of my life.

CHAPTER 5

The Best Thing I've Ever Encountered

The Bishop at USCC was the best thing I had ever encountered, he, and Lady Sybil J. Windriff, or so I thought. Over the five years of being at the Church I made friendships that would last into adulthood. It wasn't until I was sexually assaulted by the Bishop of USCC. Bishop Jeffery Delmont Windriff II that all I knew came crashing down on me. Yep, that's what I said, my Pastor, Bishop and "Father" sexually assaulted me. It wasn't something that just happened. Nah, it would have been too obvious. A pathological predator's job is never to be obvious, but to break down your defenses and make you completely trust them.

THE MORNING AFTER

During my time at USCC, I was being groomed, and tested and "favored"; thinking back on that time, that's what all the attention was about. I was brought close to see if I could handle seeing certain things and hearing certain conversations, and keeping secrets, even conversations we had. How else should I look at it? I arrive at the church and it's assumed he hasn't groomed others before me? Well, that's not fully true he was sleeping with other women, but I am not writing to tell their story.

I can recall as time went on events that had been hosted by USCC. I can remember one event a guest comedian came to town. He was extremely handsome, bright eyes, brown curly hair, tall, and funny might I add, hence his reason for being there. Bishop Windriff sought to introduce this guest and I by telling him that I was single, in hopes there would be some type of love connection. He was good at hooking you up with someone. I guess that's the good that was in him. However, I would be hesitant to even admit that there is any good in him. Most things he did for you was done in order to give him some type of credit anyways.

Nevertheless, I am so glad that "hook up" didn't happen because I later learned this young man was pretty troubled and wouldn't have made a promising mate after all.

THE MORNING AFTER

He would have just been an extension of the abuse that I was already experiencing.

Later that night as the event was ending, Bishop Windriff and I walked to his car, and before we parted he started to tell me the things God was going to do in my life, and how I should act as a lady. He would tell me that women never chased men. That it was ok to walk in front of him and maybe flick your skirt to show interest, but you never go after a man. I never forgot that.

Looking back over the relationship, Pastor J. Delmont Windriff II, he was affectionally called, was only able to get as close as he did because my own father was not in the picture, and because I did not have a male role model in my life, at the time it made it pretty easy to take me in as his "daughter". It's wrong to assume what a person knows without them confirming or saying anything, but actions do speak louder than words. He knew this, and so to mistreat me and mishandle me would be easy because I put my trust in the man who portrayed himself as my "father".

He would tell me on a regular that he is my father. My biological father was in and out of jail most of my life. So, when I got the call that my biological Dad had passed, I was sad, and I cried, because at the time of his death he was

THE MORNING AFTER

getting out of jail, and we had promised to work on our relationship. The part that hurts me most was he asked to see me. I refused because I thought he was coming home, and so I said that I didn't want to see him laid up in that bed sick and helpless dying from cancer, and that I'd see him when he came home. Little did I know he wasn't coming home. His cancer had progressed so quickly that he couldn't be saved.

I was 21 years old when my Dad died. At his funeral Bishop J. Delmont II and First Lady Sybil J. Windriff sent one of the Parish Pastors to represent USCC. The Parish pastor came as moral support for me, and it was so appreciated and needed. It was around this time that Bishop Windriff started telling me that he is my Father now even more. He went so far as to announce it over the pulpit that I was his daughter. I can remember him saying, "Kaye is my daughter, and nobody better not bother her. He said, don't worry about a pit bull coming after you if you mess with her, you'll have me to worry about." That made me feel so protected, so loved, so included, and so looked after. After all, he did what my own father and mother had never done, and that was protected me, and speak up for me, warning others on who I was, and how to treat me.

CHAPTER 6

Being the First Female Drummer

I absolutely loved being at USCC, it was so much fun. After every Sunday service the young people would get together at one another's house. There we would eat, rest, then be on our way to evening service that started promptly at 6 PM sharp. At first, I was just a member of the church, but I later started playing the drums there. I wasn't the only drummer USCC had, but I was in rotation with 3 other drummers.

Being the first female drummer at USCC wasn't so hard. I was still a beginner drummer and it helped a great deal that there were other drummers better than me. This helped me sharpen my skill to be with other drummers

THE MORNING AFTER

that could play better. I was able to learn from them and to be challenged just about every Sunday. The lead worship leader, at the time, was tough and she didn't hold no punches when it came to the musicians of USCC. If on a Sunday morning you weren't playing the drums on beat, or was too slow, she would switch you out! It could be in the middle of shouting music or a song, it did not matter! She didn't play.

That was the most embarrassing thing that could ever happen in a church full of at least 200 people, AND the drums are at the front of the church too! How embarrassing. I got switched so often that instead of me getting bitter, or upset, I made it my goal that I wasn't going to get switched anymore. I worked hard at building my stamina. I learned to stay on time with the beat, and to keep up with the other two great drummers. I was getting better and better. Until one Sunday, a new drummer joined the rotation and he started getting switched. It was the best feeling in the world to know that I had "arrived" at the standard of that worship leader, that she no longer switched me out.

As I grew in playing the drums, and as I grew in the word with the youth group, we'll call this group Youth Group Therapy or YGT. I learned that there was a call on my life,

THE MORNING AFTER

but that it would be a couple more years before I would accept this awesome call.

Within YGT, many of the young people dated, and hung out with one another. I wasn't any of the boys age, so I didn't date anyone within the group, but there was a young man that wanted to talk to me outside the YGT. I was still young, and dating was not my thing. As this young man tried to get my attention to let me know he was interested in me I was fearful, and clueless that he even wanted to talk to me.

As I became more involved in the church, I was interested in becoming an adjutant; so, I went into training. An adjutant, for those who are not familiar with this position as it pertains to the church. It's like an armor bearer or assistant. You are assigned to a person of high ranking in the church and you serve them. You serve them in any capacity, you carry their items, or help them get dressed whatever this leader needed, you were assigned to help them. It could be one of the head leaders like a Pastor, the First Lady, or one of the Mother's or Deacons, or one of the Bishops.

I wasn't assigned to any of the high-ranking leaders because First Lady Sybil didn't like me too much. This wasn't told to me until later how much she hated me. The words that were told to me later after I left the church was that "she couldn't stand me". Unfortunately, the feeling was not mutual. I honestly looked up to her and love her dearly. Being a young lady, I looked to her, to glean and learn, but was able to learn from afar though. What I was able to observe was how well she served her family and cared genuinely for her children as they were growing up. I especially paid attention to how she served as a leader in the church. From my view, she was always smiling and laughing. She was pleasant and charming. Many people were taken by how pretty she was as well. You have to remember, I was not allowed to get but so close to her, so my view may have been a bit distorted.

However, one really huge event hosted by USCC every year was a convocation. This was when all the churches affiliated with USCC would come together, it was more or less like a big church family reunion. Most of the young people from the host church would be assigned to someone.

So, let me explain why I was not chosen that year to serve as an adjutant. A few months before there was an event at the park for the church. The young people were having fun, playing games, and throwing water balloons. The Bishops and Parish pastors that work in the church were there as well. We started playing with the water balloons and water guns. Someone started throwing the water balloons in my direction and so I ran to keep from getting hit. As I am trying to dodge the water balloons, I held on tight to one of the Bishops in order to stop the water balloon from hitting me, and it hit him, and much to my chagrin, we ended up falling on the ground together. Bishop Windriff thought this was hilarious, but First Lady Sybil was furious; that Sunday after service she called me into her office to reprimand me and let me know that I was being "silenced."

For those of you that don't know being "silenced" is when you are sat down or excused from your position, all duties and responsibilities in the church for a certain amount of time. It could be months before you are reassigned. When you are sat down, you are being watched closely to see if you misbehave during your time of being "silenced", and if you do mess up, your time is extended; and when your time is up you resume active duty; because of the water balloon event, I had been silenced.

Months had passed, and I thought that I would have started training to serve by now. I was told by Bishop that I wouldn't be sat down too much longer, and that I could start to get my garments to serve. I was on my best behav-

THE MORNING AFTER

ior, and others were getting ready for the Convocation. I remember distinctly having a conversation with Lady Sybil via messenger. I was super excited because I thought I was being released to serve and I shared this news with First Lady Sybil. I can remember her response being, "Oh"? I guess Bishop Windriff hadn't shared this news with her yet, and I spoke too soon.

The next thing I knew two girls who were like little sisters had been acknowledged openly that they would be serving in the Convocation. I was told that I was still being silenced from being an adjutant. Instead, I was assigned to one of the Mothers. We'll call her Mother Georgia B. Handel.

Mother Handel liked me a lot, and I liked her. I served her so well that she gave me a set of pearls that I still have to this day. Others would look at this assignment as a dummy assignment, one that was not of importance, because the Mother was slow and not in high ranking status. She was just one of the Mothers of the church who needed help getting from point A to point B. I can honestly say, being in a position others would make fun of was humbling for me. Serving Mother Handel taught me patience, compassion, and how to care for someone of her status. Although, I was hurt at first because I thought I would be able to work

THE MORNING AFTER

in the actual convocation as an adjutant, but I did end up serving Mother Handel at the convocation and thereafter.

So, the convocation came, you have to understand, being a part of the Holy Convocation was huge for us. My little sisters and I roomed together during this year's convocation and it was so hurtful seeing them get ready while I just sat there. I recall one day during the convocation I saw Bishop sitting in a restaurant. The restaurant has a huge window so you couldn't miss anyone who passed by. As I'm walking by I waved at Bishop Windriff and he motions for me to come in. What's so funny, those were his exact words as I walked over to him. He said, "come in, ya look hungry." Laughing, I sat down and refused any food, but did get something to drink. The conversation was casual, I was asking him about how he thought the convocation was going so far and how he was enjoying himself. He smirked and said, "How are you enjoying the convocation?" I told him it was ok. I did not dare mention why I was not serving like he said I would, because I didn't want to start any argument with him and First Lady Sybil. So, we talked causally. I can remember him telling me a story about how secure Lady Sybil was. He said, if she walked up here right now and saw you and I sitting here together having breakfast, she wouldn't be bothered at all. Or if

THE MORNING AFTER

I told her that I had breakfast with you, He said, she'd say, "how is Kaye doing?" I thought that was an odd conversation to have, but nothing he did was too close to normal anyways. But then he starts to share with me how some of the women he comes in contact with have taken advantage of his kindness.

CHAPTER 7

It's All Just a Game

He told me a story once about a woman who came upstairs to his office in a fur coat with no clothes on and exposed herself to him asking him to "just touch me". I'm thinking in my head as he is talking, he *really* trusts me if he's telling me this. Not thinking at all that this is an inappropriate conversation to be having with me. This was an attempt to gain my trust, my loyalty, my commitment to him. Thinking, "I'll tell her a secret and make her feel special or make her feel that she's trustworthy". It was all a game to him.

However, I was later told by Bishop Windriff that I was going to be trained to be his adjutant, that I was going to be the first female adjutant to serve him, but that he was watching me. He said he sees a bit of goofiness in me and that he was watching me. If you knew the type of person Bishop Windriff was, you would understand why that was such a big deal to be his adjutant, and his first female adjutant at that. He was revered and honored. If you spoke ill about him, his followers would literally crucify you. Oh, trust me, I know, because I was one of them.

Just Like Family...

The years at USCC was so much fun. I had a church that felt like a family, and a Papa that felt like a real father. It was great! I was in rotation playing the drums. I was no longer silenced, but I was told that I would still remain the adjutant of Mother Handel. I was building healthy relationships. I had even joined the dance group that had started. Let's call this dance group "Shabach Praise & Dance Team." We danced on special occasions like Christmas, Easter, Mother's Day, events like that. It was a lot of fun.

I can remember one day Bishop Windriff came to the church during one of the rehearsals. During a break from dancing, I went upstairs to say hi and get a hug. He was in his office working as usual. In this particular conversation, he told me that his daughter really looked up to me, and that I was like an older sister to her and he asked me if I would protect her and watch out for her. "Yes, sir" were my words. I was so happy that my Papa trusted me with his daughter, and that she looked up to me. Again, being a person with low-self-esteem at the time, this made me feel good, and important. So, from then on, I made it my duty to protect her. Now, whether or not all this was true about her looking up to me, I couldn't tell you. It was all of what he told me, and because he was my "Father", I believed him. I had no reason not to.

Bishop Windriff had a way with words. He could get you to believe just about anything. He was an awesome storyteller. He can deliver the toughest messages or have the most difficult conversations with ease. He would hit you with words and you would not even realize that you were slapped in the face. He was my role model, and I looked up to him. He was my hero in a sense because I had never had a male role model treat me like I mattered and like I was special, or like I counted and was worth protecting; Bishop Windriff did all that and more. After everything happened and thinking back on the one on one time, I can't help but to think he was grooming me. I can see why his wife didn't like me.

Side Bar

Let me be very clear, Bishop Windriff and I did not spend a lot of time together. He didn't personally come to my home and pick me up or call me on the phone regularly. We did have phone conversations, and we did spend time together, but it would mostly be when he or I was at the church. I was a student in school at the time, so I wasn't working a day job, and his job was at the church, of which he spent the majority of his time.

His wife did an excellent job making me know I was accepted, even if she didn't agree. Her "pretend face" was the only thing I knew to be true when it came to her. I say pretend face, because thinking back on the encounters with her, she never gave me a sign that I wasn't liked by her, so I say she has a wonderful "pretend face". Her communication with me was pleasant but brief. It was her I wanted to get to know not Bishop Windriff, but she would never pull me close. It never bothered me though. I thought that was just how she was, pretend face and all.

CHAPTER 8

A Test of my Integrity

One year I received a phone call from Bishop Windriff; it was a general conversation, like most of our conversations were. He talked, I listened. Then one day, he called and as he talked the conversation felt more or less like a test of my integrity. Have you ever talked with someone or dealt with a person that would not ask you for something but would be suggestive? For example, someone you know needs to borrow some money and they won't ask you directly, but will mention in conversation what they need, and you feel obligated to offer them what they are suggesting? Ever have that happen to you? Well, this particular conversation Bishop Windriff did this to me.

THE MORNING AFTER

It was one evening, I was home, he called and asked how I was doing? I told him I was fine. I asked him how he was doing? We got on the topic somehow of me being a single woman and how it would look if people saw us together out in public, what they would say and how it would be perceived, especially if we went on a trip, he said. I said, well if you keep what you know to yourself, and I keep what I know to myself, then no one would know. And he said, that's right, and did a little chuckle. We talked some more, then we hung up. I remember calling my mother to tell her what just happened, because it was unusual, and my mom said, that's weird, why would he say that? I was like because he's my Papa, so going on trips with him or riding with him in a car was nothing to me. I didn't view it as anything other than he is my Dad, and we are having a conversation.

TRIP ONE:

Two weeks after that phone call we went out of town. It was just he and I and it was over night. I stayed in one room on a totally different floor, and he stay in his own room on a totally different floor. My thought was hmmm, why are we on two different floors? What's the big deal, but I had to remember, I was not Bishop Windriff's biological daughter and to keep anything from looking weird and suspicious, and to protect our reputations, it would be best that we were on two different floors. Now, at least this is what I told myself; nothing out of the ordinary happened. It was a good and safe trip, we went, and then came back. He didn't drop me off at home, but to my car that was left at the church.

TRIP TWO:

A month or so after this trip myself and another Civil Air Patrol member (CAP) rode with Bishop Windriff to the base in Columbus. In 1999, I joined Civil Air Patrol as a Cadet Airman Basic, then branched off to teaching the kids known as the Pre-Cadets (not a part of the military). They weren't a real group, they would never go to service, it was just away to involve the children that were pre-school age, and kindergarten ages. They learned the basic rules to Civil Air Patrol, the Military alphabet, we would meet weekly and just have fun. It was a fun way to learn the military rules and regulations.

Bishop Windriff was the Chaplain of C.A.P. So, he took me and another Cadet to get our uniforms. They are called Mess Dress and BDU, which is short for Battle Dress Uniforms. We're in the car, I'm in the back seat while the

THE MORNING AFTER

other Cadet is in the front seat and they are having a general conversation. Nothing stood out about the conversation. I was reading a book that had just come out by Bishop Jakes titled, "The Lady, Her Lover and Her Lord". My thinking was that I have time to talk to Bishop Windriff whenever I wanted so I didn't feel left out of the conversation because we had them all the time. I can remember the Cadet just talked and talked and I can tell Bishop Windriff was getting a bit annoyed because she was one of those know-it-alls, but he did well and never let it show.

A few months went by the trip to Columbus was good. We went, got our uniforms for a dinner that was coming up with the Civil Air Patrol and we each went home. I can remember one-night Bishop Windriff called me again. The conversation started off pretty general; he wanted to know how I was doing? I had entered school around about this time, so we discussed that. Then the conversation slowly moved again to me being a single woman and him being a married Pastor and what would people think if they saw us together? At this time, he introduced to me taking a trip and he wanted to know if he could trust me. In my mind I am a bit baffled that he had to ask because we had taken two trips by this time, but I had to remember Bishop Windriff was not my biological father, and no matter how much he lets everyone know I was his daughter, I was still a single woman and he was a married Pastor. So, he was assured, again by me that he could trust me and that I would be glad to go. As we continued the conversation Bishop Windriff starts to talk about how he's in need of a great massage, and how great he is at giving them. Then he goes on to rant and rave about how others have said how great his massages are. We talked a bit more and then we hung up.

TRIP THREE

On this trip we were scheduled to stay overnight. One of the deacons and the Church secretary went down with us, but they came in separate cars. I rode with Bishop Windriff.

(Side bar)

If I may pause here and say that my friend's mother-in-law, Mrs. Dee, is a devoted woman of prayer. A few days before going on this trip I received a phone call from my best friend saying that her mother-in-law said for me not to go, that something bad was going to happen. I remember saying to her that, that was impossible, He's my Papa he wouldn't hurt me. I remember her saying in a sad tone,

THE MORNING AFTER

"ok, but call me when you are leaving so I can know that you are ok." I assured her that nothing would happen and said ok.

CHAPTER 9

Rickenbacker Base (Columbus, Ohio)

The ride to Columbus Rickenbacker base went ok. The conversation was normal, nothing was said or done out of the ordinary. The ride was going great. At some point, Bishop Windriff received a phone call from his wife Sybil. So instead of staying overnight like he'd planned, we were going to go back to Cleveland once he finished business in Columbus. I heard him say to her, Ok, then I'll come home. I am not completely sure why we were going to the Rickenbacker base, but I do remember we did a lot of paperwork and cleaning. After a few hours of cleaning, later that evening Bishop Windriff told the others that came down with us

THE MORNING AFTER

that we would be right back, that we were going to go get a bite to eat. We rode to the Embassy Suite Hotel. Bishop Windriff made reservations at this hotel because, remember, we were staying overnight. As we are pulling up to the Hotel parking lot, Bishop Windriff said, we'll stop and get a bite to eat. He goes to his trunk and pulls out his suitcase, and we walk to the room he has.

I can still remember what it looked like. When you walked in there was a small love seat on the right side of the room. On the left was a table for two, in the second part of the hotel room was two beds with a television sitting in a cupboard. Before you reached the bedroom, you would see the bathroom on the right side.

We walk in and Bishop Windriff goes straight to the bathroom and run the shower. I went in the room and sat on the bed. I sat on the bed because it was just a natural thing to do for me. I walked in with Pastor and just followed him. He went into the bathroom. Surely, I wasn't going to follow him in there, so I went to sit on the bed until he came out.

Minutes later Bishop Windriff comes out and says to me, "I want to give you a massage." I looked confused and dumbfounded all at the same time. My ears couldn't

THE MORNING AFTER

believe what I just heard him say. I remember the conversation we had concerning him being a great masseuse, but I didn't want a massage from him. What do I do? What do I even say at this point?

I'm scared and confused. It had not dawned on me that he got the room for an overnight stay so he could "massage" me. I didn't think we would be in the same room any way because of the trip we took to Pennsylvania and we stayed on two different floors. It was my belief that we would eat, he would get some rest, and that we would go back to the CAP Rickenbacker base.

I'm screaming in my head, somebody help me! Somebody help me! My thoughts became a blur, I was trapped. In fact, those were the words I heard when he said that, I heard "TRAPPED" and then I saw a black bird cage fall down over me, but instead of the size for a bird, it was my size. I instantly went to the age of eight years old when I was first molested.

I was taken into my Grandmother's basement and placed on a worker's table, I call that table a slab because it felt cold and dark, and I was afraid. No one came for me. I felt trapped then and I felt trapped again in this hotel

THE MORNING AFTER

room with this man. Now he was no longer my father or Papa or Bishop or even friend; he was a molester, a violator, a predator or in my eight-year-old mind, "a mean man".

I could not tell you how long we were in that room it felt like an eternity. All I could remember was the penetration with is fingers, let me pause here and explain. THERE WAS NOT PENETRATION BY BISHOP WINDRIFF WITH HIS PENIS. His penis was not working properly, he suffered from prostate cancer years back, and so his man part was not functioning like a healthy man's would. That did not stop him from using his two fingers and massaging my entire body from top to bottom, front and back. I laid there with my eyes closed tightly, scared and afraid. At one point I opened my eyes and he looked like he had the face of a dark demon, he was unrecognizable, and he was grunting. To see that made me shut my eyes even tighter.

I'm on the floor with the two couch cushions from the small couch in the front room when there was a knock at the door. Bishop Windriff had ordered room service. He goes to get the food, I am assuming he places it on the table, because my eyes are still closed. I can hear him shifting and moving around in the front room. The door closes and he comes to "wake me up" he doesn't allow me to get

THE MORNING AFTER

dressed but he wraps me in a white sheet in what he calls "Roman style" this is when one shoulder is out of the sheet and the rest of the body is covered.

CHAPTER 10

Keysha, Are you Alright?

We are at the table and my mind is in a complete blur. I could hear Bishop Windriff talking but I couldn't tell you what he said. It was like the teachers in the cartoon Charlie Brown, were all you heard was wahhhh wahh wahhhh wahhhh wahhh. I remember eating something sitting at the table. I do not remember getting dressed, but I remember walking out of the Embassy Suite Hotel room, and he said to me, "DON'T CUT YOUR HAIR ANYMORE, YOU HEAR ME? He suddenly turned mean and harsh towards me. I can only liken it to the story with Tamar and her half-brother Ammon in the bible II Samuel 13. For those who don't know the story, Ammon lusted after his half-sister, the Bible says he fell in love with her, he faked sick in order to get her to his bedside then raped her. After he raped

THE MORNING AFTER

her the Bible says in II Samuel 13:15, "Then Ammon hated her exceedingly, so that the hatred wherewith he hated her was greater than the love wherewith he had loved her." (KJV)

We drive back to Rickenbacker base in complete silence, He's talking but I cannot tell you what he is saying; the rest is a complete blur. I do remember on the ride back to the base it felt like I was floating to the top of the inside of the car, like I was having an out of body experience. I could see myself, and I could see him talking to me. As we pull up to the base, I hear him saying, I'm gonna take this to my grave. I hear myself say, "huh, oh yeah… me too", then we walked into the base and it was business as usual.

My best friend called me as I'm standing at the base on the phone surrounded around the members who came with us. I couldn't talk so she did all the talking. I can remember her saying, "Keysha, are you alright?" There was a long pause before I said, "No". She then said, call me when you get home. And I said, "ok". I felt like a zombie, like I wasn't in control of my thoughts or actions. It was all just a blur.

When it was time to go home, he told me to ride back with one of the other members that came down to the

THE MORNING AFTER

base with us. I can remember I talked the entire ride from Columbus to Cleveland. As we are driving, Bishop Windriff rides next to us and looks over at us. He's on my side of the car and all he does is look then he falls back behind the car we are in. He does this like four or five different times until we arrive back at the parking lot of USCC. It was the longest and scariest two-hour ride ever.

The member I rode back with was so kind, she listened to me talk and talk and talk and talk. Something I do when I am nervous.

Help! Can somebody help Me

Once I got home, I don't remember calling my friend back. I don't remember much of anything that night. Only that I got home and crawled under the covers. I couldn't cry. All I could do was lay there. It was like I was in shock.

After, I got up the next day and things went on like normal. I was still one of the drummers at the church, so I had to go to choir rehearsal that week. I can remember being at rehearsal and screaming in my head, SOMEBODY PLEASE HELP ME! CAN YOU DISCERN HOW HURT I AM, CAN YOU SEE HOW DIFFERENT I AM ACTING? At one point during rehearsal Bishop Windriff comes in. I immediately hid my face behind one of the cymbals. I didn't want to see him, and I didn't want him to see me. I started losing my cool, started flippin' out and acting weird, so much so that the choir director asked me what was wrong with me, and that I needed to get myself together. After that Bishop Windriff left the rehearsal. It was as if he was checking up on me. He's never come to one of our rehearsals before.

It all Felt like Make Believe

My friend's mother-in-law, Mrs. Dee, wanted to know how I was doing. She was running a bible study at this time and she asked me if I wouldn't mind coming. I went only because she asked me. She tried to do some sort of intervention for me, but it didn't work. I had not spoken to anyone concerning what happened that night because I was still in shock, and everything seemed so distant to me, like it was make believe or a dream, like it didn't happen.

Mrs. Dee did a pretty ok job keeping up with me. I still had not said anything to anyone because I myself was still trying to make sense of what happened. What made him think that was ok? Did I do something or say something that made him think I wanted this? He knew about me being molested as a kid and the trust issues I struggled with. What possessed him to think that was ok? It felt like he gained my trust to the point that when he approached

THE MORNING AFTER

me, he knew I wouldn't resist because of the respect I had for him.

One evening me, my friend and Mrs. Dee went for a ride to the park. There, she just let me talk, because I still had not spoken to anyone concerning what happened. As I am starting to talk, I'm getting extremely angry and then I start to cry and ask "why did he do this to me? What made him think this was ok to do to me?" I remember crying and crying. My heart was so hurt, my mind was so confused. I remember thinking, no one is going to believe me, only because of who he is. No sooner after I said this to myself, I get a call from Bishop Windriff. He wants to arrange a meeting with me. I agree to meet him, but I agreed to this only to go get my things from the church.

Mrs. Dee, said, "there's no way I am letting you go back to that church". She and my best friend were in the car when the call came through from Bishop. I told Mrs. Dee he wanted to meet in his office, she hatched out a plan and told me she'd go with me. I was a drummer, so I had to get my drumsticks, and a couple other things.

CHAPTER 11

I Looked Back One Last Time

On the day I'd decided to meet with Bishop, I had prepared a letter to give to him. It detailed all that he'd done, and how what he had done made me feel. I'd discussed that how he knew my past and how I'd been abused, mis handled and how I didn't have an active father. Asking him how he could do this to me knowing the trust I had in him. I explained how violated I felt by what he did, and fully understanding that he was not my biological father that maybe that's why it made it so easy for him to hurt me.

I remember walking into the church, the door was already unlocked, and Bishop Windriff had not gotten there yet. While Mrs. Dee waited in the car, I went to retrieve my things from the basement and from the drums. I walked

THE MORNING AFTER

upstairs to Bishops office. I didn't open the door; I only slid my letter under it and then walked to the other side of the church and slid a copy under Lady Sybil's door. At the bottom of my letter I wrote to him I cc'd Lady Sybil. I thought that once he read the letter and saw that it was cc'd to Lady Sybil that he'd go to her office and try to get it, but I emailed the letter to her as well; to ensure she knew what had happened on April 4, 2001. I remember feeling so scared and nervous. I was afraid that Bishop would show up before I had the chance to get all my things. Once I got everything, I looked back one last time, and from that day on I have never looked back.

The ride to my home was nerve wrecking. I can't tell you how spastic my thoughts were. It was evening time and once I got home, I checked my email to see if Lady Sybil had responded. She didn't respond to the email, but we did messenger. She spoke first. Her question to me was, "Tell me, did he take advantage of you, or did you let him touch you?" It felt like she was in a hurry to get my answer. Like I needed to tell her my side of the story really quick before Bishop came home. I'm not sure if that was the case or not, but that's what it felt like. She came off concerned, then suddenly, like within minutes, she got really nasty and mean. I'm thinking Bishop Windriff must've come home; because her conversation then went to, "well you're always in his face, I can see why what happened, happened". I messaged back to her, "No I didn't LET him do anything and I'll serve you notice that if anybody else puts their hands on me again they will FUCKING DIE!" I clicked out of the conversation and I haven't spoken to either of them since.

He Ran Like He Saw a Ghost

I did have a few encounters with them accidently after that. I can recall being invited to an event with a friend of mine, he was a journalist. We walked in and sat at a table. He had to work the room to get his story, so I was at the table alone. The way I was positioned at the table I can see everyone come in. The place was pretty big so there was no way I could have seen everyone from where I was sitting. I was looking at the agenda and when I looked up, I see Bishop Windriff walking around greeting everyone. He saw me, we saw each other. My heart pounded so fast, but I remained calm and cool. When he saw me, I'd never seen him walk so fast away from a table it was as if he saw a ghost and got startled. It was almost comical.

THE MORNING AFTER

The night went on, he stayed on his side of the hall, and I stayed on my side. I didn't want him to makeup another lie and tell the people I was trying to talk to him at the hall. Like he did when I slid the letters under, he and Lady Sybil's door. He told people I was trying to get in touch with him and with his children. He even went so far as to say that one time when I was asked to go to his home to get a deck of cards, actually it was the time the church had the outing and the water balloon fight broke out. Lady Sybil asked me if I would drive her car to go get some playing cards that was in the nightstand next to their bed. He tells the story that when I went to get the playing cards, I laid on his bed and fantasized about being with him. What lies!

As I started to look around the room, I started noticing the people at the event were members of USCC. I suddenly started feeling a chilled eerie feeling in the room. I hadn't recognized anyone until now. I hadn't even recognized one couple, actually a couple that was in the Youth group with me when I was a member of USCC, he and his wife sat at the table with me and had a conversation with me. As members would come in, the women would just look down their noses at me. They wouldn't speak, they would just stare, then turn their heads to act as if they didn't see me. It was hurtful, but not as hurtful as the day

THE MORNING AFTER

he told the young people from USCC not to speak to me. Not to communicate with me because I was spreading lies about "their Pastor".

CHAPTER 12

The Encounter

The process for me after that was very difficult. Funny though, my relationship with God's people was destroyed, but not my relationship with God. Some way, somehow, I still loved God, but I wondered, what I had done to deserve this? I had decided that I would never join another church. That people are just mean, evil and bad. I knew that I wanted to stay connected, but I would never again join another congregation. I could not take being mishandled again. I wouldn't give another leader the opportunity to misuse me and abuse me again. I would go to church but joining was something I couldn't see myself doing EVER!

There was another Bishop that used to be affiliated with USCC but they left for whatever reason. I went under this church's covering. The Pastor and First Lady were outstanding. They had heard rumors of what had happened and when I arrived you could tell they wanted to protect me. I never had to tell them what happened, or hint to how really messed up I was mentally after this ordeal. I could feel this protection in how they handled me. They didn't get too close to me but allowed me my space. It felt like I was in a spiritual daze. I couldn't see straight or get my bearings.

Former members from USCC were also at this Church, let's call this church God's Place of Refuge. At God's Place, I was covered and protected. The other former members had heard as well, and they rushed in to protect me too. One particular former member was an Elder at USCC, and she and I became really close friends. She was older, so she more or less was like a mother figure to me; I loved her dearly. We spent lots of time together and I have to admit she helped me through a lot of depressed days. Days when I felt suicide was the only answer to get away from all this pain and hurt.

I can recall one day we were on the phone, and I disclosed to her my plan to get revenge on Bishop Windriff and his entire family. She said to me, "Keysha, he's not worth it, he's not worth it". As I am hearing her words, I can feel the rage I had inside me to make him pay for hurting me. The anger that just builds and builds as he told lies about what happened and how after the assault how I was trying to contact his children or come up to the church to see him. All lies!!! This particular day she said, "May I pray for you?" I reluctantly said, "yeah" I could hear her words, but my heart was still on getting even.

Now, I knew that I would go to jail, and probably have spent a lot of time there, but the rage and pain I felt, it did not matter, my only thought was that he would be out of this world, and that he could not hurt anybody else, and if I had to be the one to suffer so he couldn't hurt anyone anymore, then ok. The Elder was there for me. She was my anchor; she was my hero. She was a light for me when everything went dark. After she was done praying for me, she told me that all day today she wanted me to just say "Thank You Jesus" all day. She said to just say those words. So, all day that day I would say, "Thank You Jesus." It changed my mind about taking revenge on him and his family. The relationship with me and the Elder continued on, even after I left God's Place of Refugee Church.

I can remember many people wanted to hear what happened, but only for the reason of taking what I said back to him, in my opinion. I was completely distraught, and alone at the time it happened. I suffered for a while with nightmares, and night tremors thinking that he was coming for me. I can recall having this one dream of being in this house that was under construction. There was scaffolding and plastic covering like 80% of the house. I can remember seeing Bishop in my dream, and I remember walking up to him and asking him "why did you do this to me, why?" He looked confused and lost and he said, "I don't know, I just don't know." To this day I truly believe he didn't know why he did what he did to me.

I wanted so badly to have someone in my corner to talk to, to talk to me, to let me know that I would be alright. Unfortunately, it did not turn out that way. The young people at the church weren't talking to me, and that hurt the most. Only because I thought they were in my corner. I thought we had built a friendship. They each may have had their own personal thought or opinion of what happened, but their silence spoke volumes to me. It told me that I was in this alone, and that whatever story they were told by Bishop Windriff, they believed.

I remember this person (Adrianna) who was like a mom to me at the time, but now she's more or less like an older sister. She did try to reach out to me, but I was so afraid of anyone who affiliated themselves with the Windriffs, that

THE MORNING AFTER

I didn't trust anyone coming from that circle. However, I didn't get the story of what happened until I left.

Adrianna tried and tried to reach out to me, but like I said I just didn't trust anyone who came from that circle of people. We saw each other at an event years later. We switched numbers and it just went from there. She did later explain that she did believe me, and that if I'd only talked to her, she would have told me. I don't think it would have mattered then anyways. I think that at the time we started talking was the time God had ordained. I was really in a bad head space after the whole ordeal, and because I had trust issues, I don't think it would have made that much of a difference.

CHAPTER 13

Why Go Back After God told You to Leave?

There was a lot of pain, and confusion on why this had to happen to me. I had suffered a significant amount of abuse felt like all my life, and I am healing and working on issues. How could this happen, and by someone I completely trusted. He was my Bishop, my Pastor and Father.

I later learned that The Elder that was so kind and generous to me at God's Place of Refuge went back to USCC. It completely crushed me. I felt in my heart that when she returned, she shared what we discussed with Pastor Windriff, but why? Why go back after you said God told you to leave? That part, I didn't care about, what I was most concerned about was the information I shared with The

THE MORNING AFTER

Elder in trust, in confidence. I was devastated. I saw The Elder a while after that, and I had nothing to say to her. I was so hurt, that I could not put into words how I felt. It felt like another blow by someone I trusted. That love that I felt for her turned into hatred, total hatred.

CHAPTER 14

I Won't Be Silent No More!

For years no one could know the truth about me; because if they did it would change how you treated me. It would change how you talked to me. No one could know that I suffered some form of sexual, mental and emotional abuse from the age of eight years old to forty-two years of age, and that even though I am in an adult body, I was a scared little girl wondering who she is. For a long time, I couldn't talk about this without breaking down, or without stopping in the middle of telling it because I would be so overwhelmed with emotions. First being ashamed and afraid to tell because people would not believe this man, this clergyman, did this to me. Not understanding that Clergy sexual abuse does exist and it's not just in other denominations but can exist in any place where the spirit of perversion, and sickness lives.

It has become so clear to me that "Men of God" or "Women of God", are human FIRST. I Corinthians 15:46-47 says, (MOUNCE) "However, the spiritual did not come first, but the natural, then the spiritual. The first man was of the earth, made of dust; the second man is of heaven." This simply means that God has an order to everything He does in the earth, and this follows that order. We are not born spiritual; we are born flesh with all its idiosyncrasies and sin. So, it makes sense that man would be subject to the fallen nature of this world.

The Sleep Over

I can recall one event at the age of twelve years old. A family member came over and ended up staying overnight, and he slept in the same bed with me. Now this family member was a lot older than I was. That night he tried to touch me; he didn't get far, I felt him pull my panties down then try to stick his penis in my behind. I woke up, pulled my panties up and went into my mom's room to sleep with her. That morning I went to tell my mom, she was in the kitchen standing in front of the sink when I told her that Bruce (not his real name) tried to touch me. From what I could see there was no expression on her face. She didn't acknowledge what I said, she didn't say a word, we just stood there with her back to me the whole time. hat made me feel like I had no value to her, that I had no voice, that I had no protector.

People meet me now and ask why am I so self-sufficient why am I so independent, why don't I depend on anyone, let someone help you; I was never able to do that. After that moment in the kitchen with my mom when she failed to come for me, I decided right there, at the age of twelve years old, that I will be my own protector. I made a declaration that I will have my own back. No one's going to watch out for me, so I am going to watch out for myself, and I started making that declaration out loud standing right there in the kitchen, I just kept saying, "NO ONE HAS MY BACK, I GOT MY OWN BACK, I'M WATCHING OUT FOR MYSELF".

I was suspicious of everyone and didn't let anyone get close to me. I did have someone that got close. I always say, she saved my life. I believe God had it in His plan for me and this person to meet. I believe she was born for the purpose of being my friend. When I talk about her, I am happy and all the memories of the hurt and harm go away. It was as if God used her as a safe haven. For a long time, she felt like a security blanket, like a safe place or shelter. She didn't care, at that time, that I was mean and snappy. It didn't scare her that I never smiled and that I had no friends. The things I suffered, without her being in my life, I believe I would not be here today if it weren't for her. I can remember when we were about the age of eleven or twelve, we were playing in this field like area and this man walked up to us and just started a conversation with us. We were talking about superheroes and so he started talking about superheroes with us, and I thought I was Wonder Woman.

So, the man walks over to me, places his arm around me and says, "Oh, so your Wonder Woman huh?" but as he's doing that, he touches my breast. I remember pushing his arm away from me, and just walked away. It seemed there was never a time I was not in the grasp of dirty perverted men. I can remember once we lived on a street called Hillsboro, and the landlord would stop by periodically. This one particular time, I was home alone, and the Landlord kept making passes at me. He would use the excuse that he was coming to "check" on us.

CHAPTER 15

Start Talking my Friend

I've learned now, Ma'am, Sir, with years of therapy coupled with prayer, support and healing, I do not need anyone to validate what happened to me. I do not need anyone's approval on what happened, and I definitely don't need anyone to believe me. I lived it, my body remembers it, even if some events are not as clear, my body does remember, the emotion is real. The flashbacks or "PTSD" is not made up in your mind, and that's proof enough for me!

When I got to a point where I would start talking or at least mentioning that I was assaulted, I used to tell my story and look for people to validate it. I used to look for someone to believe that what I was saying is the truth, that this man really did do this to me. He really did place his hands on my body, and in my body, or feeling like I needed someone's permission.

Now, after years of contemplating what to do, and learning that I am no longer a victim, my testimony is being told not from a victim's perspective, but a survivor's perspective.

I encourage you to start to tell your story. Don't be fearful because it may not have been something like someone penetrating you. Abuse comes in many different forms and happens on several different levels. Some survivors are never penetrated, but they have been sexually abused. So please, don't feel that your story is insignificant or small compared to someone else's because of the act or lack thereof. The most important part is that you survived it! You made it, and now it's time to heal.

Healing is a Process

Understanding that sexual predators come in all shapes, colors, sizes, personality types and professions. It is sad and hurtful that they can come also as your teachers, your coaches, your Pastors, or Priests, your family friends, babysitters, or family members. It is my understanding that church is supposed to be a place of refuge, a place where people can go to get help, or direction spiritually. Church is supposed to be a place where all the ugliness of sin and burdens can be laid in exchange to feel some sense of direction or normalcy. Church should be a place where people are PRAYED for instead of PREYED on. When the institution of church becomes what the world is, where are we safe?

Healing is a process for me. When I testify that I should be dead, in a strait jacket or in jail, I mean it! I am still processing even as I write on these pages. There are still areas of unforgiveness that I struggle with; I struggle with forgiving him, and the family members that harmed me, but I am learning that forgiveness is not for the other person, but that it is for me, and that in order for me to walk fully in my purpose, I must forgive all those who have mishandled me in any way, shape, or form.

As a part of my spiritual training, church has taught me how to cover up. How to pretend everything is "ok" by the clothes you wear, by the position you hold, by how well you praise God, or "shout" or by how well you keep secrets, and even now, I am thinking that because I am a believer in going to church and because I've been through sexual abuse, it is expected that I say that I am healed, and I forgive, and everything is just fine! Well, it's not! And I struggle with forgiving, although forgiveness is my goal. I must be honest with you in where I am. Does that make me any less of a person who loves God? Or any less of a representative of Christ? In the words of Paul in the Book of Romans,

"God forbid" with sexual, mental, and emotional abuse in my past, I can see that I am a work in progress and although forgiveness is my goal, I have yet to fully accomplish this, but I'm not giving up. I understand that hurt people hurt people, and even though it hurts and causes a great deal of pain. This one thing I can do, and that is no longer be afraid of the faces, the words the accusations or the process.

When I think about it sometimes, it does make me angry! It makes me feel like I want to hit something or scream to the top of my lungs WHAT MADE YOU THINK THIS WAS OK TO DO THIS TO ME!!!!!!!!!!!!!!!

I have to say, that it's a tragic and heartbreaking to be taken advantage of by someone in authority. Unfortunately, they do come in the form of a family member, a pastor, a family friend, a counselor, a boss, or even a complete stranger. It destroys boundaries and it shatters your self-worth and confidence. If you don't have the right support group around you to affirm you, or to rebuild you, to believe you or even protect you, it can be devastating trying to cope and live in this world with what's been done to you.

I can start to understand that people who prey on innocent children or seek out people to abuse or take advantage of have once been people who were hurt, mis handled or abused at some point in their lives. And just because you stand in a pulpit, and wear a backwards collar, does not make you exempt. The unfortunate part is that they didn't get the help they so desperately needed to heal properly.

For anyone that's reading this book and if you were taken advantage of, mishandled or mistreated by leadership, I want you to know your life is not over, and you are not damaged goods. I sometimes struggle with that if I had gone forward in pressing charges against Bishop Windriff, other girls or boys or women would not have been violated after the event happened with me.

A few days after being sexually assaulted by Bishop Windriff, I was taken back to Columbus by a friend. She drove me the two whole hours to the Columbus police station where she encouraged me to file a report and press

THE MORNING AFTER

charges against Bishop Windriff II. We go in together to get the process started, but the officer would not allow my friend in the back with me to take my statement. I remember being in the huge room. I felt cold, and terrified, because I didn't have the support, I needed in the back room with me. It was just me, the officer taking my report and the big round table.

I tell my side of the story and as I am talking the officer is writing. After he gets my statement, he says, "ok, so now we are going to go call this man to let him know he will be having charges pressed against him" I totally lost it. I don't even think the officer got the full sentence out of his mouth before I said to him, "you're going to call him?" The officer says, "yes". I remember saying, "oh no! please, you can't call him" The officer then says to me. "You mean to tell me; you are a twenty-seven-year-old woman and this man sexually assaulted you?" The smirk on his face told me that he totally did not believe me. He closed his pad and got up from the table where we were sitting without saying anything else to me. If he called Bishop Windriff or not, I do not know to this day. I was shaking so bad that I could feel my skin trembling; I was so scared and terrified. I decided not to go forward with pressing charges.

THE MORNING AFTER

I am aware that there were others though. I cannot remember how I got connected with this female detective, but I can say when she started working with me, she encouraged me to go forward. She could not give me names of his other victims, but she hinted that there were others that were fearful and did not come forward. I do struggle with that part of what happened to me. That I wasn't brave enough; I just couldn't do it. I was convinced this man had more power than the police, and that even if I pressed charges, he would still find me and hurt me in some way.

CHAPTER 16

In Retrospect

In retrospect, I have decided I will remember the good things we shared and cherish them. I will think on them often and take it as an opening for new beginnings and a life of adventure and exploring. I will take each moment, explore it and learn from it. I will forgive myself for not being brave. I will not suffer from the regret of anything that did not occur but will take that which did occur was meant. I had fun and enjoyed each moment. For those times that were hurtful, I explore those as well. I embrace it and I use it to make me better, to explore who I've become after the hurt, the heartache, the waiting, or whatever else made me question who I am, my self-worth and my value. I am grateful for today and I position myself to be loved and to live out loud. I do not regret the time I spent, or the

THE MORNING AFTER

moments taken, it was all for my good and God will use every moment to make me better.

I can say that now only because of the healing that has taken place. I have put in the work, and for me this journey will be ongoing.

The years have passed, and so has Bishop Windriff. The events that occurred some twenty years ago is still being remembered, but in different ways. Some events I remember still make me angry. Some events I remember warm my heart with forgiveness. Nevertheless, I live a victim free life on purpose. How do I do it? Every day is different, you would think that because he is gone, that I would no longer struggle, or that I would be relieved. No, it took me wanting and needing to be free spiritually, mentally, and physically to live a productive victim free life. I not only had to work on forgiveness of one abuser, but three. Some days it had become a challenge to live the life God intended for me to live before the plan of the enemy came to pass. The journey does get difficult sometimes, but it doesn't stop me from living.

As a Mental Health Therapist, myself I understand the importance to have someone in your corner to talk to. This person may come in the form of a Therapist, Pastor, or friend. Having that positive, safe space to begin the process is important.

    When I heard of the passing of Bishop Windriff I remember I exhaled long and slow... It was as if my body was holding on and at hearing the news, it just let go on cue. I didn't know of what I was even letting go of. I thought I had done all the exhaling. I thought I did what was needed to recover. It was as if an elephant were sitting on my chest, and just decided to get up. It was as if I started to thaw out. That's a weird way to say it, but this is the only way I can describe it. I felt like I'd been waiting to exhale...breathe... live.

My Prayer for you my Friend

My prayer for each person that reads this book, is that you begin your journey to healing. Seek professional help in order to walk you safely through the process or find someone you can talk to just to start putting into words what you have endured. Someone needs to hear your story. Each story of abuse is different, there is something in your story that can help someone to connect or start their healing. I pray that once you start to speak it across your lips that you become strong, vigilant and fearless in letting others know your story, always remembering that a secret loses its power once it's told. Tell your story...

> Heavenly Father,
>
> I am asking that you heal the person that is reading this book. I am asking that as he/she begin to put the pieces of their life together that you let them know that you are with them, that you are present and that you will walk with them as they bravely face the fear that keep/kept them in bondage. I pray that they will come to the realization that you are bigger than their fears, and that it was not their fault.
>
> It is my prayer Father, that as they start to talk about the trauma that you would come in like a flood, and lift up a standard against them, that you will be a healing balm to them as they process and make sense of what happened. I ask Father that a hedge of protection will be around them as they safely process, and safely go through this healing process. We rebuke all shame, blame, guilt, and fear. May the Lord Bless you and keep you, In Jesus' name I pray,
>
> Amen.

REFERENCES

https://www.rainn.org/statistics/victims-sexual-violence

Psychology Today.org

Made in the USA
Columbia, SC
04 June 2021